To Jesus, who cares for all,
from the mightiest king to the tiniest mouse. Thank you.
—K. W.

To Tiphanie, Barnaby, Joshua, and John
—J. C.

SIMON AND SCHUSTER
First published in Great Britain in 2005 by Simon & Schuster UK Ltd
Africa House, 64-78 Kingsway, London WC2B 6AH

This paperback edition first published in 2005

Originally published in 2005 by Margaret K. McElderry Books
an imprint of Simon & Schuster Children's Publishing Division, New York

Book design by Sonia Chaghatzbanian
The text for this book is set in Bembo
The illustrations for this book are rendered in acrylic paint

A CIP catalogue record for this book is available from the British Library upon request

ISBN 1-416-90409-3

Printed in Italy

1 3 5 7 9 10 8 6 4 2

Mortimer's Christmas

Karma Wilson ★ Jane Chapman

SIMON AND SCHUSTER
London • New York • Toronto • Sydney

In a big house
lived a wee mouse
named Mortimer.
He dwelt
in a dark hole
under the stairs.

Nobody ever noticed little Mortimer.
And Mortimer liked it that way.
But he didn't like his hole.
"Too cold. Too cramped. Too creepy,"
squeaked Mortimer.

Each day he sneaked out
and crept about looking
for crumbs and tidbits.
One day . . .

Mortimer spied something new. What he spied was wonderful!

He saw a huge tree covered with
twinkling lights. Nestled on top
was a bright, shining star.
But something even better
than the tree itself sat next
to it on a table. Mortimer
sighed with delight.
"A house just my size!"

But the house was so high
and Mortimer was so low.

"I'll climb up the tree,"
said Mortimer.
It made a perfect ladder . . .
for a mouse.

Up, up, up
Mortimer climbed.
Down, down, down
ornaments crashed.

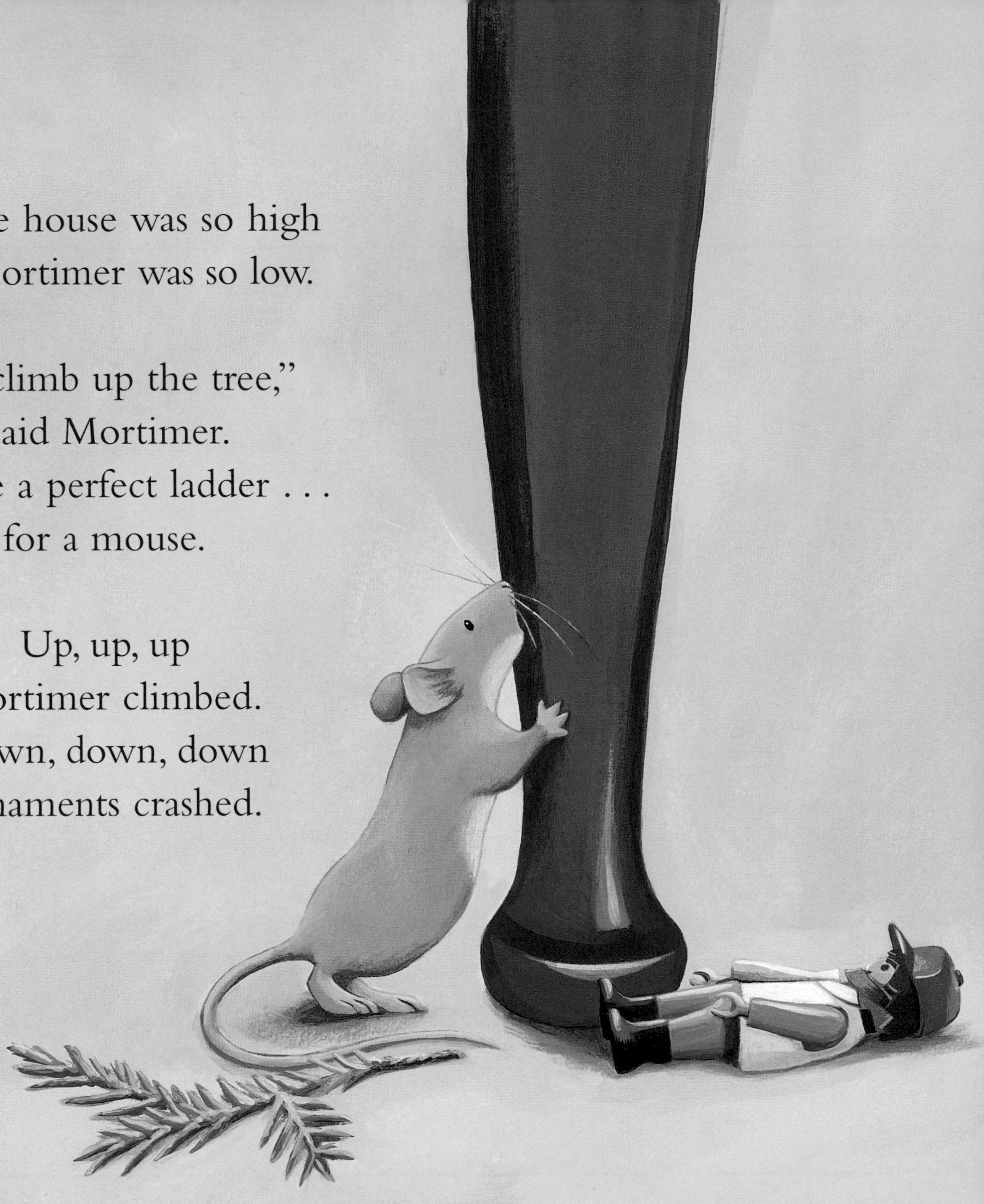

Finally he reached the table.
"Perfect," said Mortimer. "Not cold. Not cramped. Not creepy. Cosy! But – who are you?"

Mortimer had never seen people so small. Almost as small as himself. He had never seen such strange animals, either.

Tap . . . tap . . . tap . . .
Mortimer knocked, but no one answered.

Tap . . . tap . . . tap . . .
No one moved an inch.

"I see," Mortimer squeaked. "You aren't real! Only statues!"

And so, Mortimer lugged . . . and Mortimer tugged.
One by one he dragged the statues out.

When he reached the smallest statue, he saw it was . . . a baby.
A baby in a wooden bed just Mortimer's size.

"There's no room for you here,"
Mortimer said. "Out you go."

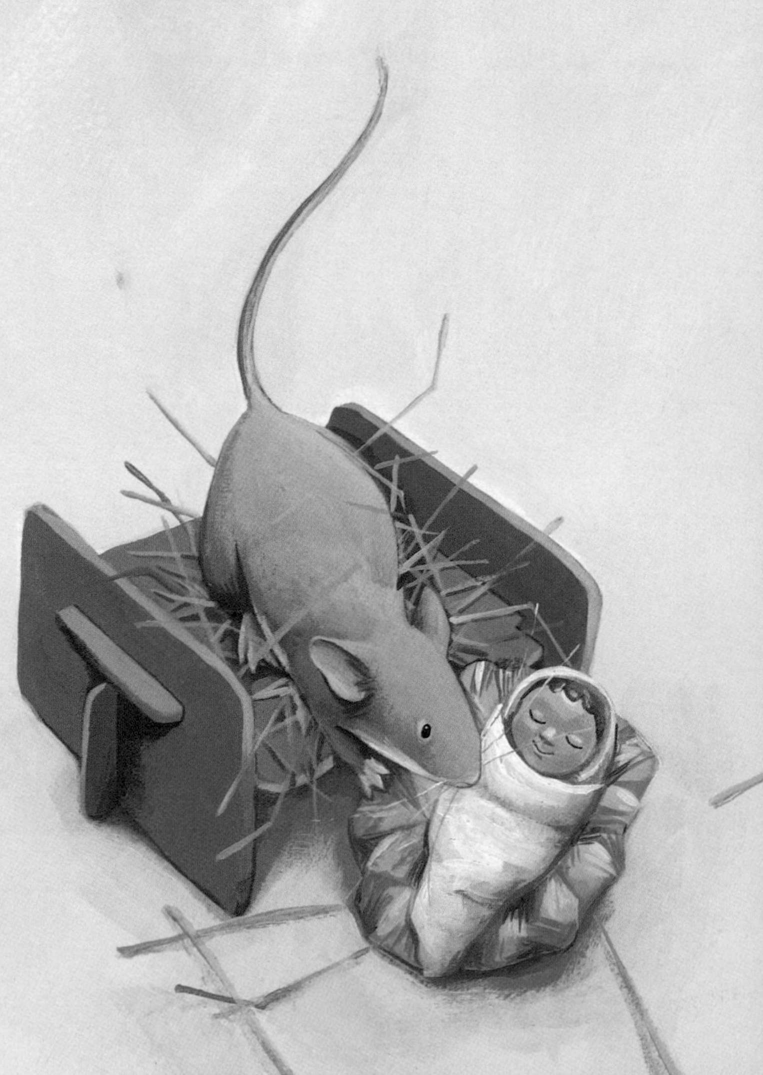

Then into bed crawled Mortimer.
He fell fast asleep in the soft, warm hay.

The next day, as Mortimer crept about,
he found good things to eat.
Biscuit crumbs, fruit cake morsels
and spicy peppermint sweets.

But when Mortimer
scampered back up
to his new home,
the statues were
set up again.

"No,
no,
no!"
squeaked Mortimer.
"This won't do.
There's no room
for me!"

And so . . .

Mortimer lugged . . .

and Mortimer tugged . . .

until all the statues were out.
"And stay out!" he said.

Then into bed crawled Mortimer.
He fell fast asleep
in the soft, warm hay.

But each day, while Mortimer scurried about,
the statues were set up again.

And Mortimer
always lugged
and tugged them
back out.

Then one day . . .

Mortimer set out and saw the big people gathered around the tree. He couldn't go out there, so he hid among the statues. A man started talking.

Mortimer listened. And what he heard was wonderful!

"Since it is Christmas Eve, I shall tell the Christmas story," said the man. *"A long time ago in a little town called Bethlehem…"*

Mortimer heard about people named Joseph and Mary and a bright, shining star. He heard about shepherds watching their flocks by night and travelling wise men. The man continued…

"And there was no room for them in the inn."

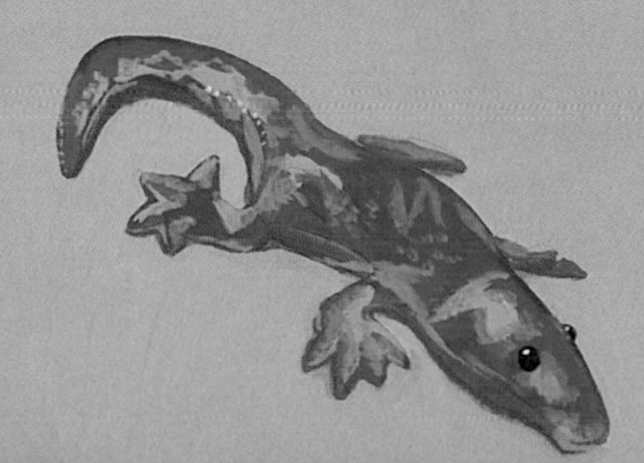

Then Mortimer heard about a baby.
A baby who was born in a stable and had
no real bed but slept in a wooden manger.
A baby born to save the world!

"And the baby was called Jesus," said the man.

Mortimer looked at the
bright, shining star on
the tree. He looked
at his new home
and his new bed.
He looked at
the statues.

Last of all, he looked at the baby.
"I see . . . ," sighed Mortimer.
"You aren't just any statue.
You are a statue of Baby Jesus."

Mortimer sniffed.
Mortimer snuffled.
A tear rolled down his furry cheek.
"There was no room for you in the inn.
But I know where there is room," he said.

And so . . .

Mortimer lugged . . .
and Mortimer tugged.
Soon he dragged all
the statues back to
where they belonged.

Last of all, he laid the baby in the manger.
"This belongs to you," he said.
Mortimer smiled.
"You look warm and cosy now."

There was no place for Mortimer
to go except back to the cold,
cramped, creepy hole.

As Mortimer scuttled down the
tree, he said: "Now that Baby
Jesus has a place to sleep, maybe
I could have a home, too?"

And then Mortimer
spied something new.
What he spied was wonderful!
Mortimer sighed with delight.
"A house just my size."
There were no statues in sight.
And so . . .

Mortimer moved right in.
"Thank you, Baby Jesus," said Mortimer.
"You've made room for me, too."